I REGRET CHEATING ON MY WIFE.

Angel oliver

DEDICATION
THIS BOOK IS DEDICATED
TO ALL COUPLES OUT
THERE GOING THROUGH A
ROUGH PATCH

CONTENTS

BOOK TITLE

ACKNOWLEDGMENT

I wish to Extend my special thank to my
family and friends ,who helped me alot in
finishing this book,within the limited time.I
am Making this book not only for Mark also
to increase my knowledge.
THANKS AGAIN TO ALL WHO
HELPED ME.

BOOK TITLE

I regret cheating on my wife

CHAPTER I

My name is gabriel, I am from lagos state, married to a very beautiful and loving woman. She is forty-four while I am fourty nine. We met more than fifteen years ago in the U.K, dated for two years, and have been married since then. We have three children, and we relocated to Nigeria, theee years ago. Coming back to Nigeria was due to the type of business I started, after I quit my job.

I love my wife so much, more than words can say, and I always go out of my way, to make her happy. She's not perfect, just like I am not perfect, as well, but I love all her imperfections. She's the woman that completes me. We are both doing well for ourselves, in our different fields.

I cheated on my wife with my twenty-seven years old secretary, who is my wife's cousin.

BOOK TITLE

I regret cheating on my wife

This is something I never ever thought I would do to my lovely wife. I am someone that is strongly against cheating. I didn't know what came over me, that made me not to think straight.

It was my wife that insisted I gave her the job, as she wanted a family member working for me, than someone she doesn't know. In always wanting to please my wife, I did not object. There weeks into the job, I noticed that my wife's cousin started dressing provocatively to work, I didn't read too much meaning to it, until the day she brought home made food to work, to serve me, during lunchtime.
The first time she did it, I politely turned her down. I didn't understand why she would serve me food at work, not like I had ever complained to her that I wasn't getting good food, or something. When I got home that day, I told my wife what happened .

BOOK TITLE

I regret cheating on my wife

Gabriel   honey,   something   funny
happened at work today

BOOK TITLE

I regret cheating on my wife

Bella what happened

Gabriel your sister served me food at work.
I was surprised , tho I turned it down

Bella Why na She told me about it and I
gave her go ahead. She thought it would be
best to be bringing you food, once in a
while, so that you will be eating good food
during lunch. That thing your neighbor sells
and calls food, is po!son. I'm sure she will
be feeling bad now. I'll have to call her later,
to apologize

Gabriel Oh, is that so I didn't know,You
should have told me. The food smelled
really nice, it was serious self control that I
used   to   reject   it

Bella smiling .I will tell her to bring for you,
tomorrow. I just hope she will have the

I regret cheating on my wife

strength to go through the stress again. That girl can cook . If not for my health, I would have continued waking up very early to prepare food for you to take to work. Not to worry babe, be managing for now, till   I   can   start   again

I also wanted to tell my wife to talk to her about the way she dresses to work, but I let it go, I didn't want to start sounding like a woman   that   gossips.

That was how it started, two times every week, I would eat a well prepared meal from my wife's cousin, that is my secretary. I didn't read any negative meaning to it. I was actually enjoying it, she was a very good cook, just like my wife. I guess it's a family thing.

This continued for two months. Then one Sunday evening, I had a major misunderstanding with my wife that made

BOOK TITLE

I regret cheating on my wife

me storm out of the house in annoyance.
My first time of leaving the house like this
since I got married.

I regret cheating on my wife

Chapter II

It was six pm, when I left the house. I had no place in mind I was going to. I just drove out in annoyance, got to a junction and parked inside the fast food there, and waited. I had hoped that my wife would call me to apologize, so that I will go back home. This was something that has never happened before, not the misunderstanding part, though. That one happens on regular basis. What I mean is that I have never left the house because I was vexed, never, since I married my wife.

I sat inside my car for more than an hour, no call came in from her, which made me angrier. I started going through my phone contacts, to see if I could call one of my

I regret cheating on my wife

guys, to meet me somewhere, maybe to
drink a bottle or two, while I wait. I was
still checking, when I received an sms
from my secretary. Which read ...

Good evening sir, how is family, sir Please,
I would like to know if you are okay with
me bringing you party rice tomorrow. I
forgot to ask you on Friday. Regards to
mummy Tope

That was it. I didn't think twice, I called up
my secretary, immediately after reading
the sms... dunn dunn... she picked up
after the second ring.

Secretary hello ,good evening, sir. Hope
you got my message, sir

I regret cheating on my wife

Gabriel   Yes, I did. Can we meet That is, if
you are less busy

I regret cheating on my wife

Secretary sure, sir. I am not doing anything, I can come to the house as soon as possible. Hope everything is okay, sir

Gabriel don't want you to go to the house. Meet me at that hotel in T-junction. I'll send you the address via sms, call me when you get there

Secretary okay, sir. I'll be on my way

I wasn't thinking straight anymore. I was so angry at my wife and it blinded my sense of reasoning. In my twisted mind, I felt the only way to punish her was to cheat on her. I didn't know what I was thinking. The whole thing happened like a flash. My Secretary, who happens to be

I regret cheating on my wife

my wife's cousin, didn't pause to ask me why I wanted her to meet me in a hotel. She agreed to meet up, without any reservations, whatsoever. I sent her the name of the hotel and address, like I said.

The hotel was where I lodged my friends that visited me from the UK the month before.

I drove into the hotel and went straight to the reception to book a room. Fourty top-five minutes later, I got a call from my Secretary, that she had arrived. I gave her the room number and told the receptionist to give her a pass.

I still didn't think I was making a mistake.

BOOK TITLE

I regret cheating on my wife

It hadn't clicked in my head to retract my
steps. My wife still hadn't called.

I heard a soft tap on the door and went to
open it. My Secretary was dressed like she
knew what was going to happen. She
looked at me as she walked into the
room, without saying a word. After
locking the door, I took long strides
towards her and pounced, like a hungry
lion that has seen a willing prey. She
made it very easy for me. To my utmost
surprise, she had no undies. As we were
way into it, my phone started ringing. At
first, I ignored it, but when it kept ringing
non stop, like the person was determined
to kill my battery. I got off to see who it
was. It was my wife

I regret cheating on my wife

My junior that was standing very tall, dropped instantly. I broke out and started sweating profusely. My Secretary laid there and was staring at me with eyes that was eager for me to handle the phone and quickly get back to business. It was at that moment, I realized my mistake. All the anger I was feeling, left me. I stood there for a few seconds, looking at the phone as it rang.

Oh, God. What have I done

I finally gathered myself and picked the call ...

Bella My king. The man after my heart. I am deeply sorry, please, forgive me and

I regret cheating on my wife

come back home. I have been trying to
reach you since you left, but the network
wasn't helping matters. You know how
this place can be, especially during
weekends. It's difficult to make a decent
call. Are you there Say something, please

My heart broke in thousand pieces.

Gabriel i thought you won t call. What
you said to me wasn't right at all

Bella I know , I'm the one calling you to
apologize, am sorry. I don't want to make
any excuses for my actions earlier. I take
all the blame, forgive your wife. You
know I'm the only you have. Or do you
have another person

I regret cheating on my wife

Gabriel No, I don't. I just wish you had
called me like an hour ago

    Bella but I just told you I've been trying.
Immediately you left the house, I gave you
thirty minutes to simmer down, then I
started trying to reach you.come back home
please , You surprised me ,The way you
stormed out of the house like something
was pushing you. I asked myself if it was
only what I said or there was something else
I did in the past that you harbored in your
heart

Gabriel bella,bella God You should have
called earlier. You should have called
earlier. You should have called
earlier,bella

I regret cheating on my wife

Bella i hope you are okay What's going on I don't understand the way you are sounding

Gabriel don't worry, I am coming back home.

I ended the call and turned to look at my Secretary with distaste.

I regret cheating on my wife

CHAPTER III

As my secretary saw the look on my face, she got up from the bed and started picking her items from the floor, including her handbag, I don't remember how it managed to land there. Someone that looked attractive to me few minutes ago, suddenly looked like a ghost.

Gabriel please, nothing happened here, absolutely nothing. Inviting you here was a big mistake and it doesn't change anything between us. I don't want us to ever talk about it. My wife is your sister, I'm sure you know how much this would hurt her, if she ever gets to find out

I regret cheating on my wife

BOOK TITLE

Secretary Sir, please I don't understand
what is going on. You called me, I came
and delivered exactly how you want it, or
you didn't enjoy it.

Gabriel are you okay Enjoy what You
know nothing happened, you are talking
about enjoyment

Secretary nothing happened Something
happened, sir. The time you were using
your fingers to caress me, weren't you
enjoying it If not for that call, your junior
would have gone in, you were ready for it
and I was also ready, nobody is a baby
here

Gabriel okay, my fault. I am very sorry for

I regret cheating on my wife

everything, it won't happen again. This one shouldn't have happened in the first place, thank God we didn't go all the way. Here, take this for your transport and stress.I gave her a reasonable sum of money.

Secretary thank you so much, I appreciate. Please, drop me off at the junction, let me take a bike. Just so you know, I don't regret what happened, Infact, I enjoyed it. Let me know when you want us to finish what we started, I'm sure you will be the one always rushing back for more after you taste the main soup. I know I am sugar and honey together

I regret cheating on my wife

xx

Gabriel I would rather you leave the way you came in, please. I gave you a lot of money, use it to get an uber or something, I won't drop you off anywhere, it's not safe for me. I have to quickly rush home now

Secretary okay, sir. Not an issue. See you at work, tomorrow

We were both fully dressed by the time we finished talking, I walked out of the room and went straight to my car, to head home. Since I got married, I've never cheated on my wife, it hasn't crossed my mind before.

I regret cheating on my wife

I didn't know how to calm my heartbeat that was racing so fast, as I was driving home to face my wife. I decided to talk to someone about it, someone I could trust. Jerry was the only one that came to my mind, he is someone I can trust, any day, any time. I parked by the roadside and dialed his number … dunn dunn… dunn dunn.

Jerry bro, how's it going

Gabriel jerry, I swear, it's not going well . I don fuck up like this I almost land my Secretary for hotel a few minutes ago

Jerry wait, wait. I don't get it. Land your Secretary as how

I regret cheating on my wife

I narrated the whole incident to him, from the misunderstanding I had with my wife to how it ended with my Secretary in a hotel. To my utmost surprise, he started laughing, I got confused ...

Jerry Finally, you have eaten the forbidden fruit, welcome to the club. Don't tell me this is the only reason you are panicking

Gabriel Jerry. E reach to panic . I said I've never done such to bella before, she doesn't deserve this treatment from me, and please, I didn't eat any forbidden fruit, we didn't go all the way. We were about to, when bella started calling, right on time.

I regret cheating on my wife

Jerry maybe that's why you are feeling this way. You didn't plug your junior, I suggest you replan with her on a later date, and have it to your satisfaction. We have all done it , it's not new, all man dey do am. I love my beautiful wife a lot, but that doesn't mean I don't collect from outside, every now and then. Okay, let me tell you my latest sin, maybe it will make you feel alright. You remember Bukky that year in school.

Gabriel sure, that fat one. I heard she's married with kids now

Jerry yes, she married way before us sef. I finally had her after all those years of her denying me. That is not even the gist, last

I regret cheating on my wife

weekend, I had her daughter also the girl is hot, she scatter my medula, and before you say anything she is an adult, twenty - three years old, sweet girl. Don't ask me how I linked up with her

Gabriel no man, that's extreme. Mother and daughter. That's not okay, at all

Gabriel You see We are in this together, mine is even worse than yours, but the world hasn't ended, has it I'm still happily married to my loving wife. Just go home, Keep a straight face and pretend nothing happened, with time, all these things you are feeling right now, will go away. Don't forget to finish what you started .

I regret cheating on my wife

I shook my head in dismay, as I listened to the dirt jerry was dishing out from his mouth.We finished talking and ended the call, but that didn't help me at all, if anything, it made me feel more terr!ble. I couldn't believe Jerry was that extreme, I thought I knew him well. Wow

Anyways, people can surprise you when you least expect it. Take my Secretary for example. She's a close cousin of my wife, but that didn't stop her from romping with me, without any atom of remorse. This is a girl that my wife vouches for, that she's a very good girl. Many things are really happening.

When I got home, my wife met me at the

I regret cheating on my wife

door and gave me a warm hug, with a bright smile on her face, teasing and tickling me, while apologizing the more. My guilt reduced before I went to bed, I slept like a baby, thinking there was nothing to worry about, after all.

But I was wrong. The following events that unfolded, almost destroyed my marriage.

I regret cheating on my wife

CHAPTER IV

When I got to work the next day, my Secretary greeted me like nothing happened, I heaved a sigh of relief. Driving to work, I had thought of so many awkward ways it could go when I see her, but to my surprise, it went well, or so I thought.

Few minutes before lunchtime, I was going through some files in my computer, when she walked into my office, without knocking like she used to, and handed me a piece of paper .

Secretary i want to thank you for last night, though, we didn't finish, but you

I regret cheating on my wife

made me happy. That money you gave

me wasn't enough, I used it to settle someone my mum was owing, I still need more for a few other things. Go through the list to see the ones you can do for me, if you are able to do all, I will be very grateful. I will be giving you anyhow and wherever you want it. Also, now that we are dating, don't you think it's better to call you by your name when we are alone? it's somehow to be using 'sir' on someone who slept with me

I was completely gobsmacked by the time she finished talking. I couldn't believe all that came out from her mouth. She wants to turn me into an atm. The list she handed to me had hair ,phone, smart tv,

I regret cheating on my wife

kitchen items, and some cash. What in

BOOK TITLE

God's name have I gotten myself into I
took a deep breath and spoke .

Gabriel where is all these coming from
It's like you've forgotten your position. If
you think what happened yesterday gives
you the audacity to walk into my office to
start making these outrageous demands,
then you must think me one of those
small boys you mingle with. If it was a
raise that you asked for, I would have
actually considered it, but this , you have
lost it. Take this out of here, before I lose
my temper

I flung the paper towards her, it landed on
the floor, and she picked it up, folded it

I regret cheating on my wife

and placed it on my desk, with a wide grin

xxx

on her face

Secretary You think all these initial gragra
will scare me That's not possible , lagos
babe like me. I didn't mention a raise,
because what you pay me for working for
you is very fair, this new negotiation is
based on the fact that I am now your
girlfriend, and the earlier you start
reasoning well, the better for you. If you
want me to quit and be your full time
babe, I will. That's a good job on it's own.
Except you want me to tell your wife that
you landed me last night, and you enjoyed
every minute of it

Gabriel   blackmail right That's what it has

I regret cheating on my wife

come to, a very cheap one at that. Wait,

are you being serious? You have the mind to hurt your own sister like that.Someone that hasn't done anything wrong to you, all she cares about is your best interest, she gave you this job and has been helping your family right from when we were in the U.K. You said I landed you last night and that's not true, nothing happened between us, nothing. Why are you doing this, don't you have conscience.Or you want to end my marriage

Secretary You should be asking yourself. If your marriage ends, it will fall on your head. Let me tell you, we are the same. What you had the mind to do to your

I regret cheating on my wife

wife, I did to her as well, and she is my

sister, so that makes the two of us. As for saying nothing happened between us, it will be your word against mine, wait till I call your wife and tell her, we will then know who she will believe

I quickly figured we weren't getting anywhere with this, it's either I do what she wants or face a serious marital conflict. But then, blackmail never ends, I know I will never touch this girl again, but if I do what she wants, it will be the beginning of more demands to come. One day, she might ask for a car or something that I might not be able to afford. One way or the other, my wife will find out, if it's inevitable, then it has to be from me.

I regret cheating on my wife

Gabriel you know what It's okay. I have
your list, I will review it later and see what
I can do. Give me forty-eight hours, please

Secretary that's cool. Just let me know
when you want me, I'm always here for
you. I know It's not every time madam
has the strength to collect, that's what
happens with age, but me, I'm still very
young and fresh, with enough energy and
moves. So, Should I bring your food.This
one is very delicious, I prepared it with
enough fried meat.

I told her I wasn't interested. After she
left, I began to think of how to tell my
wife what is going on. It would break her
heart, but better now than going further

I regret cheating on my wife

to spend unnecessarily on her cousin, and she still gets to find out later, that's like adding salt on an injury. I wanted to call Jerry again to vent, but changed my mind, I already knew what he would say. That dude is a proper male slut, I found out another version of him last night, that I didn't know existed. I decided to face my fears and confess to my wife.

How I managed to get through the entire day, was a miracle. All the meetings I had, I wasn't able to concentrate at all, one single mistake turned my thoughts upside down. The fear in me was loud, my heart was pounding so fast, at the thought of facing my wife.

> I regret cheating on my wife
> I regret cheating on my wife

I lost the appetite to eat anything again, after the breakfast I had, before leaving the house. When I got home that day, I waited till midnight, my wife was already fast asleep, I had to wake her with a soft tap on her shoulder.

Gabriel bella, please wake up, there's something I want to tell you.

Bella what is this thing that can't wait till morning. It's very late

Gabriel please, sit up. What I am about to say might make you detest me

Bella Detest you God forbid. What did you do.

I regret cheating on my wife

CHAPTER V

When she saw how serious I was, she got up from the bed and went to put on the light. I started asking myself if I was doing the right thing, seeing how she stood, with hands together staring at me. It's not like I am broke, I can afford my Secretary's demands and even much more. I quickly pushed back the thought of not opening up to my wife, and decided to face the deep blue sea. I brought it on myself, I should take responsibility for my actions and illicit moves .

Bella gabriel, what did you do, Talk to me, my heart is racing fast . This thing

I regret cheating on my wife

that made you wake me up by this time. God, please. Stop making me panic, say something

Gabriel I know I don't have the right to tell you not to get angry over what I'm about to say, but I appeal to you, for the sake of our children and all that you hold dear, the unwavering love you have for me, to tamper justice with mercy Please, forgive me, even before I speak

bella now, this is starting to scare me. What is it Tell me, before I lose it, I can't handle the suspense anymore. What did you do that is so bad, that you can't just tell me Gabriel , we've been through everything together in this marriage, no

I regret cheating on my wife

matter what you did, I am your wife, talk to me, let's handle it together. What forgiveness are you asking for, or did you cheat on me

Gabriel Yes, bella. I did cheat on you

There was total silence in the room after I said that. I had gone through it, over and over in my mind, how to put it out to her ,I never imagined I would say it this way, but it came out as the answer to the question she asked. There was nothing else to say, apart from the truth. I braced myself for the worse, expected her to react angrily or come at me, instead, she sat on the bed and covered her face with her hands for a few minutes, before she

I regret cheating on my wife

spoke again .

Bella did you protect yourself

Gabriel No, we didn't get to that. I didn't
go all the way

Bella oh God. Is this the first time or
you've been doing this before now

Gabriel it's the first time, I promise you.
I've never cheated on you since we got
married, I swear. I've not been myself
since this happened. The guilt is really
finishing me, I can't live like this. I decided
to come clean to you, than for you to find
out about it later

Bella So what do you want me to do with

I regret cheating on my wife

this information now, gabriel Are we not getting it enough Or am I now too old for you I don't understand why you did this and still came to rub it on my face. What should I do Get angry and end the marriage, so that you will marry your side whore.

Gabriel God forbid, bella. That wasn't my intentions and it will never be. I don't have any side chic. I told you I'm confessing, because I feel remorseful, I didn't mean to hurt you this way, please. Bella, help me, I made a very huge mistake, I need your help to make it all go away, it's you alone that can help me

I regret cheating on my wife

I finished talking and went on my knees in front of her, as she burst into tears and it broke my heart to see her that way. I sat on the floor in front of her and let her cry. I wanted her to let it all out, before I approached her again. This woman has been there for me right from when I had nothing, someone I know that can walk through fire and brimstone for my sake. How did I lose control to this extent How I've met more beautiful girls in my life time, girls that my Secretary didn't even come close to, when it comes to class, intelligence and beauty, but I never lusted after any, not even for once.

I can't figure out how this one happened. It's not like it was the first time my wife

I regret cheating on my wife

had made me angry, she can be annoying sometimes, but I've never been this extreme. I gently tapped her on the leg and told her to stop crying, she looked at me with puffed up eyes and said .

Gabriel tell me everything about her. Don't keep a single detail out. From who she is, how you met her, the last time you saw her. I want to know what both of you did, since you said you didn't go all the way. First, start by telling me who she is

Gabriel   she is someone you know very well

Bella who is the person Doesn't she have a name

I regret cheating on my wife

Gabriel she has a name

Bella is this what you want us to be doing
This back and forth, question and answer.
Can you stop hurting me the more and tell
me what I want to know, gabriel . You see
how I've kept my cool since you dropped
this on me, I bet you expected a worse
reaction from me. If you don't like this my
cool persona, let me know, so I can show
you my other side this early morning.
Who did you do it with.

Gabriel My Secretary, your cousin.

I regret cheating on my wlife

CHAPTER IV

Bella wait, what.

I covered my face with my hands in
shame, I couldn't meet my wife's look.
Why did I let myself go this far

Gabriel i am so sorry, bella. If only you
could see my heart. You don't deserve
this, I know, but please, find a place in a
your heart to forgive me. See my knees on
the ground, I am in front of you in all
sincerity, begging you to forgive me

Bella Oh, gabriel . How could you My
little cousin of all people. You should have
picked up a slut somewhere, someone I
don't know, instead of my cousin. I could
swear that you were the last man on

I regret cheating on my wife

earth that can stoop to this level. I don't know if my heart can carry this, I don't know. I am shaking, my heart is breaking into pieces, breathing is becoming a task for me. Gabriel, why Have I not loved you enough What have I done wrong to deserve this level of humiliation and heartbreak

Gabriel You didn't do anything wrong. It was my fault, I blame myself for everything and I'm ready to pay for it, however and whichever way you want, all I ask is for forgiveness. Please, I am down on my knees, forgive me. I promise to live the rest of my life making it up to you. I beg of you

I regret cheating on my wife

BOOK TITLE

Bella when did this happen and when did it start .For how long now

Gabriel nothing started, bella. This has never happened before,I told you. It was yesterday when I left the house, during the argument we had. I drove into a hotel and called her, she met me there, one thing led to another, but we didn't go all the way. She didn't even see me completely. Your call brought back my senses

Bella Oh, just yesterday. Wow Gabriel, I am finished. I need you to leave this room, I don't want to see you or be around you now. You can even leave the house for all I care, just leave, please

I regret cheating on my wife

BOOK TITLE

Gabriel bella, please, don't do this, I am
begging you, it's the middle of the night
and I don't have anywhere else to go,
even if I did, I don't want to leave you
alone like this, please

Bella really You don't have anywhere
else to go But you were the one that ran
to your Secretary yesterday. Go back to
the hotel and call her, I'm sure she will be
at your beck and call, now that you've
given her the pass. Just leave this minute,
please

Gabriel No, bella, I will not leave.
Whatever you want to do to me, I will be
here. I will not leave you in this state, I've
done enough harm already, I just want to
make things right. I know it won't go away

I regret cheating on my wife

xlviii

like that, but I will give everything to pay for the wrong that I've done you

She started pacing the room, walked into the closet and came out. I thought she was going to get something to hit me with, but she appeared with nothing in her hands. She was crying profusely, her hair was scattered, she looked so innocent and helpless. I've seen my wife go through pains before, during labour, especially for our thrid child, also when she had a tumor removed, the pain was unbearable, but I've never seen her go through this type of pain, it was different. She looked like she was about to collapse, she didn't stop pacing the room, at some point, I got up from the floor and went to

I regret cheating on my wife

xlix

her. I expected her to push me away, but she didn't. I gave her a hug and she laid her strength on me. I staggered backwards a few steps, then held her steady in a warm hug, while she cried bitterly. I didn't do right by her at all. I made a silent promise that this would be the first and last I would put her through this, never again. Never

Gabriel I'm so sorry, bella. Forgive your husband, please. Help me to make all these go away, help me, bella. Take me as your son that has done wrong, scold me, correct me and help me fix this. I love you so so so much, and you know this. I love you, infact, I don't even know the right words that can convey how much I love

I regret cheating on my wife

you. I wish you could open up my heart to see for yourself. Forgive me.

I tried to kneel again, but she stopped me.

Bella what do you want me to do, gabriel What help are you asking for.

She said, amidst tears. ▯

Gabriel i don't know what to do about your cousin. I don't know if I should sack her or not. I don't want her working for me again, I feel so ashamed of the whole thing. I even apologized to her, but she wouldn't have it, she wants me to be

her sugar daddy and start parting with money and gifts. I am torn, bella. Please,

I regret cheating on my wife

help me

Bella You apologized to her that you did what. Did you force her or drag her down to the hotel? She knew what she was doing, she had this planned all along, waiting for the perfect opportunity to hit, and you fell right into her hands. The audacity to even make demands, my own cousin that I took pity on. I paid that girl's school fees, from year one to final year, I take care of her mother even till now. This is how she pays me back. What a life

Gabriel what should I do, please

Bella you will not go to work tomorrow. You will call her to come to the house and take some files, when she comes, I will tell

I regret cheating on my wife

her my mind. I will also invite her boyfriend and make it look like I have a surprise planned out for her, so that he won't tell her. You want me to handle this, right. Handle it, I will.

I regret cheating on my wife

CHAPTER VII

I tried to hold her again after the conversation, she told me not to push my luck. That she agreed to help me handle my Secretary, doesn't mean everything will automatically go back to normal, which I understand. It will take her time to heal of this hurt that I inflicted on her. I wasn't expecting magic or a miracle to make everything go away as soon as I confessed. I meant every words I said to her, no matter what it takes, I will live everyday, making it up to her.

The fact that I won't hear the last of it, is enough punishment for me on it's own. My wife is someone that hardly lets go, even if she forgives you, she will keep

I regret cheating on my wife

reminding you of your trespasses, every now and then and using it against you. Which makes her to have her way almost all the time, but then, which wife doesn't.I believe women are naturally built that way, they aren't the perfect creatures, but they always want things done their way, and they always want to hold on to some wrong you did to them in the past, so as to make you dance to every of their tune. A price I'm happy to pay for her forgiveness, she means the world to me.

The next day, after the kids had gone to school, my wife picked up my phone and handed it to me...

Bella ok, call her. Put it on speaker phone. Tell her to bring you some file, anything at all from the office that you might need at home, because you aren't strong enough for work today, you want to just relax in the house. If she ask about me, tell her I went out of town.

Gabriel you mentioned her boyfriend early this morning. Are you still inviting him here

Bella definitely. He's on his way here, as we speak. When he gets here, I would like you to remain in the room, until your secretary comes. When both of them are here, I will flash you to come downstairs

I collected the phone from her and dialed my Secretary's number, she picked at second ring and was so cheerful that I called. I noticed that she had dropped the sir, the formality wasn't there anymore. I

I regret cheating on my wife

didn't know my wife also noticed it.

Secretary good morning. It's so sweet to see your call this morning. For you to be the first person to call me today, it means it's going to be a sweet day

Gabriel   I won't be at work today, I don't feel too strong. Go into my office, you will see a blue file I left on the table, please, bring it to the house, immediately

Secretary Please, don't fall sick o. Me thats planning on spending this coming weekend with you. I will start coming as soon as this call ends. It's your wife in the house I wish I could quickly massage you with warm water when I get there, but if she's around, it won't be possible

BOOK TITLE

I regret cheating on my wife

Gabriel   my wife is out of town. start
coming, please

Secretary   great. Awesome. Best news
this morning. I will book an uber now, see
you soon.

The call ends and my wife lets out a long
sigh. I could see that she was struggling
not to cry.

Bella   I knew it, I knew she was going to
ask if I was around. this little girl. She has
completely lost all respect for you, and
even me. This is all your fault, gabriel . See
the way she was talking to you like you
are her long time lover, and you say you
didn't go all the way, That last weekend
was the first time, eehn

I regret cheating on my wife

Gabriel   I swear, bella. I'm saying the truth, that girl is just getting over her head with excitement, she thinks she has gotten me as her lover, because of what happened. We didn't go all the way and I've never made a pass at her or even be suggestive of wanting any intimacy from her in the past, before last weekend. she's coming here, if I had anymore things to hide, I won't be comfortable with whatever you have planned

Bella   so much for blood being thicker than water. A bad person is a bad person, blood doesn't change anything. Let her get here first

Gabriel   don't you think she'll know something is fishy if she sees you or her

I regret cheating on my wife

boyfriend immediately she gets here

Bella the maid will open the door for her
when she comes. Her boyfriend will be at
the back of the house, she won't see him
or me, until she has settled down. Just
watch and see how it all plays out

I wondered where she was going with all
these. I had actually expected her to just
call my secretary on the phone and rip her
off. The whole plan, was what I didn't see
coming.Less than thirty minutes later, my
secretary's boyfriend, Jimmy alighted
from an uber, in front of my house. I
watched him through the window, as he
paid the driver. Such a handsome young
man, but he wasn't enough for his
girlfriend, I guess it's all about money for

I regret cheating on my wife

that one. She wants to eat her cake and
have it. They got engaged on her birthday,
she wears the ring always, even while she
almost did it with me in the hotel, the ring
was perfectly positioned on her finger.
This would really break Jimmy's heart, just
like it did to my wife. If I could, I would
turn back the hands of time and make
everything go away, but I couldn't. The
deed has been done. I blame myself for
everything.

I was in the bathroom taking a shower,
when my wife came to tell me to hurry
up, that my secretary had arrived. I
thought she was going to flash me like she
said, maybe she changed her mind. I
hurried my shower, got out of the

I regret cheating on my wife

bathroom and casually dressed up, while she sat on the bed, waiting for me. When I was set, we both walked downstairs together, to meet my secretary. The shock on her face when she saw us was epic! She stood immediately, and stuttered, while she greeted my wife, twice, before greeting me, like we hadn't spoken on the phone earlier.

My wife didn't respond to her greeting, she called out to the maid, instead. When the maid appeared, she said to her.

Bella go and call that guy sitting at the back. Bring him here.

CHAPTER VIII

We both sat opposite my Secretary.
There was silence in the room, nobody
said a word until her boyfriend walked in.
She was shocked to see him. Jimmy
innocently walked to her and gave her a
warm hug, with a huge smile on his face,
and sat beside her. She finally found her
voice and spoke.

Secretary jimmy, what are you doing
here.

Jimmy your Aunty invited me . It's a
surprise, she told me not to tell you. I
can't wait to see what this is about

He rubbed his hands together, in
I regret cheating on my wife

excitement. If only he knew how the smile on his face will be wiped off in a heartbreaking way. I felt for the young man, wishing I could make it all go away, but I couldn't. They both stared at us, in expectation. I could sense my Secretary's heart pounding faster than normal. The lack of pleasantries from my wife was enough to let her know something was amiss.

Finally, my wife spoke.

Bella jimmy, thanks for coming, once again. I know you are a busy person, so I won't take much of your time. You see, I invited you here today, because your girlfriend, the person you are planning to get married to, wants to be my co-wife.

BOOK TITLE

I regret cheating on my wife

She has serious, deep rooted intentions to
share my husband with me. She went
frolicking with him on Sunday, was ready
to spend the night with him, as if that
wasn't enough, she has been badgering
him to be her lover.With the expressions
on their faces, I couldn't tell who was
more shocked, jimmy, my secretary, or
me. I honestly didn't see that angle
coming. Like, what My wife was still
speaking, when Jimmy cut her short.

Jimmy   I don't understand, ma. You
mean my babe is sleeping with your
husband, This your husband, is this a
prank or what.

Bella how many husbands do I have I am
not saying this behind your girlfriend,

I regret cheating on my wife

she's seated right beside you. Calm down,
let me finish. You have to break up with
her, as she's already my husband's
mistress. I can't have you being with her
anymore, when she's now intimately
involved with my husband

Jimmy stood up and turned to his
girlfriend, the shock hasn't left his face, he
was already breaking out sweat, even
with the ac on full blast.

Jimmy babe, what's going on here. Tell
me this is a joke, please. I don't
understand this, are you sleep!ng with
your boss

My secretary started crying, she covered
her face with her hands for a few seconds,

BOOK TITLE

I regret cheating on my wife

before speaking .

Secretary no o, jimmy, I didn't sleep with
him, nothing happened, I swear

She turned to my wife, and knelt down.

Secretary nothing happened, Aunty. We
didn't do anything, nothing happened, I
swear. It's the dev!l's work. I'm so sorry, I
beg you. Sir, please, tell them nothing
happened between us. Please, sir, don't
do this to me. Nothing happened o, we
didnt do anything.The girl that walked
into my office yesterday to blackmail me,
with so much confidence, was down on
her knees, crying and appealing to me to
intervene. I felt sorry for her, knowing
that if I hadn't called her out that evening,

I regret cheating on my wife

she won't be in this situation right now.
That didn't take away the fact that she
was already nurturing the thoughts of
entangling with me, but still, it was all my
fault, I lost control and gave her the green
light that she was looking for. I could have
prevented all these, I really could have. I
tried to speak, my wife gave me that look
that says 'keep quiet'. I closed my mouth,
and she said ...

Bella you say nothing happened, yet you
are sorry. What then are you sorry about,
if nothing happened like you said.You are
not sorry , you are just sorry you were
caught. You were coming here this
morning to massage him, thinking I was
not around. Yes, I heard you on the

I regret cheating on my wife

phone. After all I've done for you this girl,
you had the temerity, to go and strip for
my husband, my own husband. You were
not even scared. So I single-handedly
trained you in school for you to graduate
and come after what is mine. The guts,
you this girl. It was out of respect that
made me not to invite your mother into
this. Thank your stars that I am not
violent, I would have designed you , scar
you in a way that you will never forget in
a hurry

Secretary Aunty, I'm so sorry, please,
forgive me. I know I have disappointed
you, I didn't mean to. Jimmy please, I'm
so sorry. Don't leave me, please. I won't
survive this. God help me o, what have I

I regret cheating on my wife

gotten myself into. We didn't even do anything, I swear, we didn't. Sir, please, say something. Help me

Jimmy did you go to a hotel with him or not. Is what your Aunty saying the truth, Yes or no. Answer me.

Secretary yes, but we didn't do anything. We didn't. Nothing happened

Jimmy then what exactly did you go there to do with him, if nothing happened like you said? I want to hear it from you, here and now. What did you go there to do.

I regret cheating on my wife

CHAPTER IX

She opened her mouth to speak, but closed it again. Her crying turned into wailing, her voice louder than it was when this whole thing started.

Jimmy i am losing my patience. You've suddenly turned dúmb right, You that never stops talking, or has the cat got your tongue I said, what did you go to the hotel to do with your boss, since you said nothing happened.

Secretary I didn't go to the hotel with him, jimmy. I didn't. I swear, nothing happened

Jimmy Are you okay or what .You

I regret cheating on my wife

admitted earlier to have gone to the hotel
with him, now you are saying you didn't
go with him. Is this the type of person you
are Your cousin's husband, a woman that
has done everything for you, someone
you never stopped singing her praise all
the time.

The last time we were together, you kept
praying for her, that she will never know
sorrow, while you were busy planning on
how to get her husband as your sugar
daddy. This is really mean ,the height of
meanness. For the last time, what did you
go to the hotel to do with your boss.

Secretary jimmy what I mean is...He was
already at the hotel by the time he called
me to come. I didn't go with him, I went

I regret cheating on my wife
alone

Jimmy lost his patience completely, he
made a move towards her, I got up
quickly to stop him. I thought he was
going to hit her. No matter what, no one
should lay hands on another person, not
on my watch

Gabriel jimmy, calm down, please. I
know you are very upset right now, but
don't do what you will later regret,
please, I beg you

Jimmy with all due respect, sir. Get your
hands off me! I don't hit women, never.
You are one to talk .If you had controlled
yourself and faced your good wife, we
won't be here right now. You have
managed to somehow destroy my

I regret cheating on my wife

relationship of three years. Three good years of emotion, commitment, strength and time, invested in a girl I thought would be my wife. You come in all your high and mighty British accent to destroy all that I've built. My babe is being humiliated, how does that make you feel. Like a boss that you are, yes. Both of you are the same, no difference at all.

I saw the disgust in his eyes, as he stared into mine, like there was a thousand and one things he wanted to say to me, but something held him back, maybe out of the little respect he had left for me. I quickly removed my hands from him...

Gabriel Jimmy, not so .I feel so bad, every second of the day, this wasn't my

I regret cheating on my wife

intention at all. You are a man like me,
you should understand, I lost myself and
did something that is now hurting
everyone of us. I opened up to my wife by
myself, I couldn't survive the guilt any
further. I hurt my wife so much, I hurt you
as well, and I'm deeply sorry

Jimmy Did you sleep with my girlfriend

Me No, I did not

Jimmy so what did you invite her to your
hotel room for. To take book records or
what.

Me   is this even necessary,This
information will hurt you the more,
jimmy. Let it go, please

BOOK TITLE

I regret cheating on my wife

Jimmy no, sir. Please, answer my
question, since my babe is running round
in circles. I deserve to know, someone
should talk to me. I need this closure

Me I understand, jimmy. We were half
way there, almost at the verge of doing it,
before my wife called me and I didn't go
any further

He turned to my wife and said...

Jimmy Ma'am, I am deeply sorry for
everything, you deserve better, you are a
good woman. God bless you. I wish to
take my leave now, I have an important
appointment I do not wish to miss. I pray I
don't break down on the way

I regret cheating on my wife

lxxvi

I regret cheating on my wife

Bella break down. Come on, jimmy, you are a man. Strong one at that. This is so painful, but you will get over it, put yourself together and focus on your appointment. I will call you later to check up on you

He turned to his girlfriend and said.

Jimmy as for you, I don't want to ever set my eyes on you again. It's best this happened now, than after I've paraded you in front of everyone as my wife. I thank God I found out who you truly are, before marriage. Tomorrow, they'll say men are the highest cheats. Don't make the mistake of coming near me again or calling my number We are done.He left.

I regret cheating on my wife

CHAPTER X

After jimmy left, my Secretary got up from the floor and made towards the chair to sit down, my wife stopped her .

Bella what do you want to do.You want to still sit down on my chair, don't try it. The floor is where you belong, you either sit on it or stand where you are.

I felt uncomfortable. Let the girl go and end all these, but I kept my mouth shut, knowing I caused everything, I didn't want to spike my wife more than she's already spiked. I just couldn't wait for the chapter to be over. She continued

Bella where's the phone I gave to you

I regret cheating on my wife

Secretary I have it here, ma

Bella alright, remove your sim from it and hand it over to me, immediately. I didn't buy you a phone for you to use it to share my husband with me. Go and buy an iphone with your own money

That was it, I had to speak up, I just had to...

Gabriel no way . Bella. Please, you don't have to do this, you are not petty, don't take back the gift you gave to her, it's not okay, I beg you

Bella don't let me pounce on you. You say petty.See who is talking. If what you did is not the height of pettiness, then tell

I regret cheating on my wife

me what is. You can't hurt a child and expect the child not to cry, or tell the child how to cry. I bought the phone with my money, I will collect it back. If you feel sorry for her, you can buy her another one, marry her as well, while you are at it. I will be petty, oh, I will be very petty today. If I was a vìolent person, I would have beaten her the way she will never forget, but I am not, she's lucky. Even if I was, what will I do to you .I can not beàt you, I can not. Both of you deserve each other, honestly. See you, feeling like king Kong, untouchable. You are the man, you can do whatever you want and get away with it, right.Head of the family, man of the house. I wonder what your kids will say when they hear this

I regret cheating on my wife

Gabriel it hasn't gotten to that, bella, I made a mistake, I blame myself for it, I don't like the repercussions, I don't like what is happening now, but I plead with you to punìsh me all you want, let her go with her phone, I beg you.

She ignored me this time and turned to my secretary that was bringing out her sim from the phone, with shaky and sweaty hands...

Bella what is keeping you. Or don't you know how to remove an ordinary sim.If it's to rush to the hotel to lay with another person's husband, you will do it in a flash. Give me my phone, and get õut of my house. I do not want to see you anywhere near me again, ever. I have

I regret cheating on my wife

forgiven you, but that doesn't mean I want to continue being family with you or that I will ever forget what you did. I will never forget. I cut off all ties completely with you. If you dare me, this girl, I will take this further and handle it the way it will ruin your reputation

The Secretary handed her the phone and left the house in shame, without uttering anymore words. She also knew that was the end of her working for me, it was over.

It's been more than six months now. My wife forgave me and we moved past what happened, but she hasn't allowed me to touch her since then. We live like brother and sister. She moved into the guest room

BOOK TITLE

I regret cheating on my wife

and locks the door every night, to make
sure I don't go in. I understand that she
needs time, but I miss her so much, more
than words can say. I can't wait for things
to go back to the way they were. I am not
an advocate of having separate rooms.

I am still making up for hurting her. I live
every day, trying to make her happy, so as
to welcome me back into her body. It's
not been easy, but I will never stop trying.
I love my wife so much, and will never
cross this line again. Never

I got a male Secretary working for me
now.

I later heard that jimmy relocated to the
United States, and has moved on with his

I regret cheating on my wife

life. I called him shortly after the incident to properly apologize to him and also beg on behalf of his girlfriend, for him to forgive and take her back, but I guess his mind is made up. He left the country without telling her. That relationship is over, because of my lack of self control.

If it ended because of something else, I won't feel guilty, but knowing it was all my fault, will continue to haunt me.

The End.

ABOUT THE AUTHOR

BOOK TITLE

Angel oliver is an entrepreneur also a
business woman
who's love for writing can't be measured to
any other ,this is her first book being
published and still has more to come as she
is set to give real life stories of things
happening generally around the world.